dead folk

other books by katherine silva

<u>The Wild Oblivion</u>
The Wild Dark
The Wild Fall
Hallowed Oblivion
Lost Oblivion
Orchards
Dan & Andy's Scary-Oke Holiday

<u>Deadlands</u>
Undead Folk
Dead Folk

<u>The Monstrum Chronicles</u>
Vox: Book 1
Aequitas: Book 2
Memento Mori: Book 3
Acquolina: A Short Story

The Collection
Night Time, Dotted Line

dead folk

book 2
in the deadlands

by
katherine silva

SWP

Paperback ISBN-13: 979-8-218-48299-2
Ebook ISBN-13: 979-8-218-48296-1

This book is a work of fiction. Anything that bears resemblance to real people, places, or events is coincidental and unintentional.

Content warning: This book contains classism, homelessness, abandonment, dementia, blood and gore depictions, animal death, implied insect violence, cancer, dead bodies and body parts, eyeball trauma, bones, mention of needles, starvation, death, grief and loss depiction, attempted murder, physical assault, drought, alcohol, profanity, PTSD, and torture.

Published by Strange Wilds Press
Print first edition: August 28th, 2024
E-book first edition: August 28th, 2024

Cover design by Katherine Silva
www.katherinesilvaauthor.com
Strange Wilds Press Logo by MartaLeo
Cover photos courtesy of Pexels and Unsplash

PROLOGUE

Janet watched the old grandfather clock in her dining room tick time away. It was the only thing that still worked in this destroyed house: the instrument's cogs and gears grinding against one another slowly and methodically. She'd found the key tucked in her dad, Hugh's, desk drawer hours ago.

She hadn't known what time to set, but it didn't matter. She wasn't trying to determine when she was, only how much time had passed since she started it up.

Telling what time it was, what day it was was an exercise in relativity. Specificity of seconds, minutes, hours... They didn't matter in her day-to-day life anymore. But for the sake of this ritual, for the sake of everything that rode on it, she needed to know the exact moment when it happened.

Sleep was elusive. There was only anticipation; the steady drill of it as it ground its way further into her psyche.

She cast a glance toward the bedroom nearby. Not yet. No movement. She was sure she'd hear him before she saw him. That's the way the ritual always was.

The night dragged on filled with incessant ticking,

incessant thoughts that threatened to make Janet go mad. Even in the dark, her sights went to where she knew she'd left the kitchen knife sitting on the dining room table. She thought about how much pressure it would take to yield against skin; how if she poised it the right way, she could drive it long and hard into the body.

Whose body? She had a few ideas.

But knives ended things too quickly and pain was what she was after. They deserved every ounce of it for what they'd done. She'd gone through the garden shed and selected the implements she needed most to put into her father's old tool belt. She'd even managed to squeeze in a small spray bottle though it was a tight fit.

A cough brought her back from the precipice of darkness and she straightened. Soon after came the buzzing.

"Wh-what? What's going on? Why is it so dark?"

That voice. It filled her with wrath sluiced with dread. She hadn't heard it in several months and had expected she'd never hear it again.

Alas, she needed answers.

Janet stood up and crossed the room.

"Hello?" he called. "Who's there?"

"We don't have much time," Janet said each word slowly. "So, I'll make this short. I'm going to ask you some questions. If I don't like how you answer them, I'm going to cut pieces of you off. Do you understand?"

"Who is that? How *dare* you? Do you know who I am?" The effrontery in his voice did barely enough to hide the tremor beneath it.

"I know exactly who you are," Janet growled. "Seven years

ago, you took something from me: someone I cared about more than anything in the whole world."

"A patient," he whispered. "You're here about one of my patients. I understand why you're upset…"

"You understand?" Janet parroted. "You understand what it's like to hear that your father was overdosed in his sleep? You understand what it feels like to mourn him when you have no home to go home to?" She scraped one of the chairs out at the dining room table and sat. "You understand what it's like when your other dad dies of a broken heart just trying to protect you?"

"You're her," he said. "The girl with two dads. The one who tried to *kill me!*" His voice bounced around inside her head like a shotgun blast.

Janet cocked her head. "Yeah. Tried."

"So, you thought you'd go for round two, huh?" The Man snickered. "I want to die, you stupid girl. I'm dying from this cancer anyway. So, you bringing me an early demise only gives me exactly what I want."

"Huh." Janet let the word linger. "You don't remember how you got here, do you?"

The Man was silent.

The buzzing intensified.

"Didn't think so." Janet bit her lip. "What's the last thing you do remember?"

The littlest twitch in its legs.

"It…It doesn't matter!" he spat.

"Denial. Classic." Janet threaded her fingers and set them on the table in front of her. "Death will do that to you."

"What?" The word was barely audible over the droning.

"You're right. You dying gave you exactly what you wanted." She focused on its eyes. "But you forgot something. You mentioned last time we met that my family is a 'bizarre one.' 'All of that herbal medicine and pagan crap filling our heads?'"

"No…"

She heard the horror in the word he uttered and knew she'd broken through. "Exactly what do you think you're lying in right now?"

The thing looked, compound eyes shimmering green and red against the flickering candlelight as it took in its surroundings. "White, everything is shining white…" he murmured.

"I'll save you the trouble. That's a bowl. I used to eat cereal out of it, sometimes ice cream."

"No!" The Man's voice ricocheted in her skull. "No! No! Noooo!" The thing tried to get onto its legs and toppled, vibrating wildly. "Why? What is this? What did you do to me?"

"Nothing except bring you back. But I had to find a body. Can't bring a soul back without something to put it into. And there was this desiccated fly on the kitchen window that seemed almost too good for you."

The Man grunted. Whined. The fly's legs waggled in the air as it struggled to move. "Oh, God! *Oh, God!*"

Janet sighed. "We don't have time for this."

"Oh, fuck you! Fuck you!" The Man squealed. "You crazy—"

"Hey! Fuck *you*! You killed dozens of patients and your whole staff and then ran off like a coward. You deserve all of this, you miserable old fuck."

Fumbling, he buzzed in place. "Wings won't work. These bloody wings won't work!"

"Those were gone long before I ever got to you," Janet explained. "Part of the reason why it was such a perfect body. Now…" She picked up the knife. "Tell me what I want to know and I'll end it. Don't tell me and I'll start dissecting."

"He'll kill you!" The Man screamed. "He's going to tear you apart."

Janet blinked. "Who?"

"It doesn't matter," the man wailed. "Nothing matters. I'm sure he's already coming for you as we speak."

She poked the knife down toward the fly, its tip coming within centimeters of its twirling legs. "Who. Is. He?"

"Do your worst!" He laughed. "I'm all you've got! You can't do anything without me!"

"True. I need to know the names of the people you owed money to. And you're the only one who has that information. But…" She grabbed a glass jar from across the table and held it up for him to see.

The Man blubbered. The fly fell over again, its legs spasming. "You can't… You can't!"

Janet shook the glass jar full of dead insects. "I've got bodies for days."

ONE

For a while, there was peace.

For a while, Ella tended the small patch of dying land that used to be her backyard. She walked the trail that led into the trees behind her house, culled water from the shallow creek there and grew flowers. Her intention was to grow vegetables: peas and carrots.

Nights were shorter than they had been in a long time, no longer filled with nightmares, but at times with bittersweet memories. She found comfort in the stars and in an old book of poems that used to belong to her father.

Until one day, a fox appeared.

Peace became hope. Acceptance of things as they were became yearning once more.

In the mornings, she watched the creature as it padded along the creek bed, bathing in its light current. She'd track it along the dusty roads out to the railroad tracks that sometimes still sang with the distant songs of oncoming trains. She'd follow it until it reached a tunnel about a mile down the tracks and then, she'd return home. The tunnel was a reminder of awful things: things she'd put behind her.

Weeks passed. Daily rituals were made. She never spoke to the fox. She never tried to get close to it. She never tried to feed it, even though she could see its ribs beneath its rusty fur. The creature had survived this long. It belonged to the land, to the sky, and to the fields and furrows. It was not hers to command. It was not hers to save, though a seed in her mind begged her to. Nature had to contend with nature. That was her new tenet.

She had made a choice.

Ella watched for the fox in the evenings as it danced in the thick grass while chasing lightning bugs, its tail wiggling, its paws prancing among the asters and the daisies. She'd fall asleep and dream of music, of her and her father and her dad dancing to fuzzy songs on the record player.

Promise and harmony mingled.

For most of the spring, she observed her new friend.

Then one day, the fox did not show up.

She didn't panic; not immediately. After all, the fox could go wherever it chose. It wasn't human: it didn't keep schedules like one. And it had clearly done something else for a time before it had appeared at her house to play.

But as that first day grew long and hot, her mind edged to doubt. It wandered as she collected her water from the creek, as she did her daily scout of the roads nearby, as she dug up ripened vegetables in the garden. His absence—its absence festered.

She rooted herself to the house even as the sky turned pink with evening. She couldn't and shouldn't have gotten attached. She knew this. She chose to think of the fox bounding through the yellow hills in search of skittering field mice, its bright orange tail like a flame as it vanished into the distance. It brought back peace for a few hours.

Ella watched for the fox as darkness fell and busied herself with preparing vegetables. She focused on mending her clothing by a waning lamplight and tried to remember the lyrics to a song her dad used to whistle when they traversed the railroad together after the fall. It came back choppy: a word here or there. She finally pieced a sentence together before she fell asleep.

Day two was even worse than day one. Still no fox.

A part of her mind had held out hope that she'd see him in the daylight once more. But it was silent outside and the silence gnawed at her like she would at a bone if she had even that.

That day, she tore up her roots and let her wandering mind carry her feet.

That day, she ignored the smoldering itch of terror that the tunnel brought and traversed the path through its dark mouth. She remembered where she'd nearly died in it, strewn upon the tracks, pummeled until she felt rage like beetles burrowing beneath her skin. Desperation. Madness. She'd only touched those nerves a couple times: once on those very same tracks when her dad had died, the other… A night she would rather forget.

The daylight on the opposite side of the tunnel recentered her. There was a path that lead off into a field of wildflowers: a path she knew better than anyone left alive in that wretched twist of land. She didn't want to walk it again. She'd said her goodbyes to what lay at the end of it months ago.

The fox waited for her on the edge of the god-awful

town, left sprawled on what was left of the meandering road there. It did not go from hunger. At first sight of the blood, at the way its body tumbled delicately in a heap, all of her quiet simmered. She inspected it, took its soft paws, its thin, ragged pelt between her fingers, and the simmer deepened to a boil.

"Foxes are magic."

The words were not her own but she repeated them and in her head, they became an anthem. A devotional. A broken decree.

She gathered him in her arms as though she would a loved one. There were no tears. There was no trying to grasp at understanding or trying to deny what had happened.

There was only acknowledgment.

There was only retribution.

For a while, there *was* peace.

And then, there was fury.

TWO

The wandering merchants on the outskirts of town had all but left. Spring was dead and summer screamed in outset. The heat in these parts was too much and the inhabitants of the town were scarce with their own water and supplies. They didn't want to encourage the scourge of mankind who camped outside its walls to stay any longer than they had to. But they knew they'd be back eventually in the fall, like strays returning in hope of a left-out plate of food.

The taxidermist's van was still where Ella remembered it: the night she traded her fox tail for the body of a marten, the night she tried to exact revenge, the night she finally lost her father for good.

She'd tried to bury those thoughts to keep her sights set on hope and all it had done was blind her to the nature of that world now. Hope had left her unprepared and soft. That wouldn't happen again.

The tent was wrapped up, the old particle board tables folded and leaned against the side of the van. Ella had made it in time.

The taxidermist swept out the van with something that

was once a broom. Most of the straw was brittle and charred. At the sight of Ella, she stopped her sweeping, eyes deadening like the many subjects she worked on. "Didn't think I'd ever see you again, girl. Not after what you did in the spring."

Ella knew the words were sharpened, meant to shame, meant to turn her around but that wasn't an option. The fox corpse weighed heavy on her shoulder. For a moment, she wondered if she felt the tickle of a fly or perhaps a maggot against the skin of her neck. "I need something from you."

The taxidermist chuckled without humor. "You think we can still trade? You're wrong. Do you even know what your little stunt cost us?"

Ella had considered that Town might not think kindly of the outer ring after she made her escape. After all, she'd used them as cover to sneak in during the eerie quiet of early morning. She'd used their hospitality to meet her own ends. But she hadn't expected to come out of that ordeal alive either. She'd expected absolution. She thought she'd made her final choice. And then Amos had to go and ruin it all; had to make her care...

"The Town questioned everyone. When they didn't get answers, they started setting fires. It was chaos. People couldn't pack up fast enough. Only those that gave them information to go on were allowed to stay and avoid the massacre. This place became a ghost town overnight."

It was hard to imagine a place already as empty as this becoming more so. Where did ghosts go when they had no dwellings to haunt? Ella stared at the van, stared at the impeccable pieces of the taxidermist's collection, at the state of that broom. "You told them something about me?"

The taxidermist raised her hands, shrugged her shoulders. "The price was fair."

All of Ella's hatred was reserved for Townsfolk. Try as hard as she might to pinch some away for the taxidermist, she couldn't. Though they lived in a world that didn't support human tenancy anymore, people still survived. Ella had endangered the outskirt community with what she'd done that night. They'd had every right to toss her up like bait for the predator's maw.

Yet…

"What did you tell them?"

"That you brought me a fox corpse and traded it to me for something."

Something.

"You didn't tell them what?"

The taxidermist swallowed. "Food. Water. It's not as if they'd believe the truth."

But she *had* mentioned the fox; that animal specifically. So, someone had seen fit to retaliate. Someone wanted to draw her out.

Ella hefted the fox corpse from over her shoulder and tenuously lay its body down on the dirt at her feet.

"I'm not taking that," the taxidermist grumbled. "No matter how new it is."

"He isn't for you," Ella answered.

The woman cocked her head at the pronoun but before she could question it, Ella said, "I need you to tell me where I can find him."

The taxidermist's eyes narrowed. "Ella, I've already told you—"

"It's Janet now," she answered. A slight breeze rustled her hair, weaved in and out of it for a moment before settling. "Where is the Undertaker?"

Something akin to fear had wormed its way into the taxidermist's gaze. "What are you going to do?" she said barely above a whisper.

"Exactly what you think I'm going to," she said.

The Taxidermist shook her head. "You're on a devil's path, girl. If you keep following it with your witchery, you'll end up so deep in the dark, you won't ever find your way out."

Ella considered the words. She'd ventured into this darkness before: blinded by her own tears, goaded by curiosity and a sense of wanting—no—needing to belong. She'd wanted to know who she came from, understand everything her parents had been before she'd lost them.

Magic trickled in their blood. It had guided their meager existences in her childhood. Invisible like air but present. They had never flaunted it. They had never misused it. It came around here and again like birthday candles and she'd caught flickers of it before it faded into the austerity of their everyday lives.

When Amos was officially diagnosed, it dried up almost as quickly as the surrounding land.

That "darkness" was as much a part of her as she was of it.

She locked eyes with the Taxidermist. "It's Janet. Tell me where the Undertaker is."

With a shaking finger crooked into the returning breeze, the taxidermist pointed her toward Town.

THREE

Janet didn't walk through town. To do so would have been stupid. She wasn't ready to forfeit her life for the sake of some scrabbling emotionless assholes. So, she skirted its exterior. She stayed far enough away and melded with the tall grass that surrounded it. She almost became part of the undulating land and fell further away from what was left of being human. Soon enough, she was on the opposite side.

The small shack that waited for her there was nearly black in color. Perhaps it was from age, perhaps colored by the smoldering ash of hundreds of dead, perhaps varnished with the oil of bodily putrescence. A ten-by-ten-foot square with a slender metal pipe stuck through the roof to blow smoke into the intermittent gusts.

Leaning against its sidewall was a towering man a few years older than her. His shoulders and chest looked like they'd been cut from the limestone quarries nearby though he was average in all of his facial features: ruddy cheeks, a long nose and small hazel eyes.

He was the kind of person she might have seen around town once or twice as a child. The kind of boy who might have played the arcade games at her favorite pizza place while she looked on in wonder. The kind of boy who might have rung the midnight bell in Town and raced into the moonlight hills laughing like a scamp with his friends. The kind of boy who tried to steal food out of people's pantries when they were burying their loved ones. The kind of boy who might have been a comedian if he'd had a chance to smile but now all she saw was the absence of it.

He was the Undertaker. His job was to burn or bury and that was all. That was all the Town would allow him.

He ate a spoonful of what looked like lard when Janet edged out of the grass toward him. It took a moment for him to recognize her. After all, they had both changed in the years since they'd seen one another.

The Undertaker was kind once. Since he'd lost his voice, Janet wondered if he would be once more.

"You've gotten tall," she said, keeping a respectable distance between them. *What an icebreaker*, she thought stupidly. They were *both* taller.

He stared at her and set his jar of lard aside. Next to him, a shovel leaned against the outside wall of the shack. Its blade was spotted with dark stains, caked in mud and ancient dirt.

"I need you to show me where you buried him."

It wasn't framed as a request and it was clear the Undertaker understood that. His eyes squinted and he took a large step toward her, one filled with menace.

Janet stood her ground. "You want to know, don't you?" She leaned in. "You want to feel what payback tastes like but you're too scared to chase it for yourself."

The Undertaker grunted and grabbed the shovel. It was

a silky movement filled with years of practice, hundreds of times picking up the tool only to bury it in someone's torso or neck in the Deadlands.

"I'm doing this to end it."

The words were quick but they kept the shovel from swinging toward her. The statement hit in the Undertaker like she'd hoped it would. A fellow youth deprived of their carefree childhood by the death of the world. Another soul clinging to survival in the only way they could: to be of use.

The Undertaker propped the shovel on his great shoulder and turned back to his shack. From inside, he collected a canteen, a pick, and an empty sack and resurfaced.

Then, he showed her toward the Deadlands.

Their destination was a short hike from town along a road carved through limestone and edged by enormous cliffs: an old quarry where the children swam and played and fished once. They passed the first pit filled with black-green water. Debris of conifer seedlings and dead fish rested in a film atop the surface.

The trail advanced into a climb. The Undertaker remained steady. He'd likely hiked this route every day for the last seven years. The change in slope burned in Janet's calves down to her Achilles.

The great stone walls that lined their route stood three or four stories tall, shadowing them from the bright heat of midday. Despite the shelter, this walk felt like being marched through the tunnels of a fort.

Carved into various rocks along the route are faces, animals, nameless creatures likely born out of childhood fairy tales. She thought she recognized a few of them from books her Dad once read to her.

Perhaps this was where the rest of the Undertaker's kindness resided, smoothed into the laugh-lines of a convivial moon or the somber snarl of an Asiatic lion.

Finally, they reached the lot: the Deadlands. Grave markers rested in small groves amongst the crippled lookout towers, rusted chains, and haunted stone walls reclaimed by nature. Because even in a world where the selfish ruled, the Townsfolk were so scared of death that they made this refuge for their bones and cut out the tongue of a troubled youth to protect them.

It was in one of these small clusters where the Undertaker brushed aside dried bushes, the burdocks clinging to his decrepit clothing and showed her the final resting place of The Man.

The Man who had once owned a hospice center out in the middle of nowhere.

The Man who let Amos die.

The Man who she had tried and failed to kill months ago.

She remembered conversing with him in his house that night. How he'd pulled a tuft of his own hair from his head and lamented about the horribleness of liver cancer.

As if she hadn't already lost everything that was important to her when she lost her parents. As if her dad, Hugh, hadn't sold their house and home to this fucking doctor so he would take care of Amos and his dementia. As if this man hadn't ordered Amos to be overdosed because he just couldn't be bothered to take care of him anymore. As if Hugh hadn't starved to death on the railroad tracks outside of town, his body obliterated by an oncoming train.

This fucking man had died anyway.

The nerve.

Janet glanced at the Undertaker. "Well?"

His stare was solemn.

"I need his bones."

The crack of metal cutting into dry soil echoed against the stone walls.

FOUR

The journey home was slow. She carried much more in her arms: sacks full of bones, the fox, bundles of dried wildflowers, weeds, and soil…

She stopped in the train tunnel and scoured the darkness until she found the wrench she left there in the spring: her father's wrench. It was coated in dried gore, hair, and shards of bone. She tucked the weapon into her tool belt on her waist and ignored the body that had endured its violence nearby. Soon enough, she returned to sunlight on the opposite side of the passageway.

Home was not more than an hour more for her and the time passed like the tick of a methodical clock. Like the clock her dad used to time the chords of his piano work in their dining room. The clock that had sat dead on the top of the corner hutch for seven years. She lost herself in trying to remember the history of it: where did Hugh get it from? Why was it so important to him to use that and not a metronome? Where did the key for it go? Maybe when she got home, she'd search for it.

That thought elapsed as soon as the road to her house

fell into view. She passed the spot where she found a similar dead fox in the spring and all of her rage returned in a soft smolder, roiling in the base of her throat.

She dropped everything she'd collected into a pile in the middle of the ruined living room. The sky was crisp blue, clouds burning off in flutters of trailing white toward the horizon. She still had a few hours of daylight left.

Enough to visit the edge of the woods where the sweet smell of summer grass bloomed into burgeoning evergreens, where the light dimmed and fanned across the bed of orange needles underfoot like the opening of a door into a dark room.

There, she knelt at the foot of a leaning cedar tree where she ran her fingers over the bark to feel its dry veins and stared at the earth by her feet. A space she hadn't dug her fingers into in years. A space hollowed out, filled, and left in solace because that was what Hugh would have wanted. To have no reminders of the harshness of what the world had become. To rest. To finally *rest*.

"It's time, Dad," she whispered. She plunged her spade into the earth and scooped out crumbling dirt, dried grass roots, and a few wriggling worms.

"This time, it's going to work. This time."

Because this time, she knew what to do.

She knew how to bring him back.

FIVE

Tattoos are overrated.

In the beginning, Janet believed she could write the words across her skin with a pen. As long as they were on her body and she could read from them, that was all she needed to complete a ritual.

Such was not the case.

It took her scrambling through the mires of coastal trade cities, ambling blocks of tents and steaming food carts and trash-picking lots to find someone who could purportedly put ink to needle and needle to skin. And then to learn it was a fifteen-year-old who had bought a tattoo gun online before the world went belly up and learned by watching online videos…

Janet paid the fee. She let the kid scratch the words into her forearm, watched the blood roll across her skin as each word was realized. His script was terrible. His o's looked like squares; his T's like f's, his s's like 5's…

But she knew the words. She'd memorized them since Amos first wrote the poem for her. It was before he'd started to forget things, before he started wandering and losing time and himself in greater regularity. These words had meant the world to her.

And with them, she'd been able to bring him back.

But those words didn't hold the same gravity for Hugh as they had for Amos. And she needed words that would pull her dad's soul or a copy of it back from the beyond.

Janet kept her father's poetry book wrapped in his old sweater in her bag. It was stored in the closet of her childhood bedroom: the safest place she could find. She brought it out into the living room and started her arrangement.

First: candles in a circle around the middle of the floor. Second, the fox's body delicately laid over the warped boards, over the dirt and glass and ash. Third: a bone. She wasn't sure what it was, but it was small and flared out at each end and she thought it might have been part of a finger. It was the first one she'd come across when she dug into his grave beneath the cedar tree. It was all she'd needed.

Fourth: pond water. There had been a slight resurgence in the spring. Moisture had returned like hope only to be snuffed out once more by summer; by harshness. She vaguely thought of her peas and carrots and how they hadn't been watered that day.

They didn't matter anymore.

Fifth: herbs. Well. Normally, it would have been herbs. Or flowers. But her dad had been buried at the edge of the woods so she brought narrow little spruce cones, dried pine needles, and cedar leaves.

Last: tears. She couldn't cry. Against her judgment, she tried to remember how losing her dad had hit her so many years ago. She tried to remember the gut punch of awakening to find what was left of his body that gray morning on the train tracks… But no tears came.

So, she used spit instead. In it, there was loss and contempt for that loss, for how it shaped the rest of her life.

She lit her candles.

She collected her father's pen from his desk in what used to be the room he shared with Hugh and held it over the flame until it turned black. Piercing the skin hurt less than she'd imagined it would. Anger offset its pain, forced it into a basement in her head as she shaped the letters across her other arm and dipped the pen back into the flame to heat it again and again.

When she was done, the smell of burnt flesh and hot ink and the tang of blood tinged the air. Janet read the single dedication Amos had written in his book of poetry to her dad:

"To Hugh: I was lucky it was you who found me."

She poured a small amount of her concoction out onto the fox and swallowed the rest.

Janet blew out the candles and let the newfound darkness envelop her as though she were a void and it needed to occupy her space. She let it in as the curling smoke from the wicks slipped into the air toward the ceiling.

Ordinarily, she'd have gone to sleep but that was out of her grasp and there was far more to do before the sun rose.

So, Janet moved the fox into her parents' old room and placed it on the bed where they used to sleep. She returned to the living room and lit the candles again for the next ritual.

It was time to bring back the Man.

SIX

The Man said there were four who came in the dead of night like crows. No one around Town had seen them before. They didn't dress like they came from this part of the state at all; didn't talk like the local folk did.

One had a long, preened mustache that he tipped with wax. He wore a stately hat that shielded his cold blue eyes. The Man called him Steele. Steele was the ringleader of this murder of crows and money was his reason for calling.

It happened right before the Collapse. Janet and Hugh had just brought Amos to the hospice center. He'd only been there for a week and Janet was under the impression that he would get better: better was achieved in stages after all. Her father would come back to her; to them. He would be Amos again.

Steele arrived at the hospice center with his three followers in tow: a witch who was said to wield innumerable power, a young trickster with a fondness for hard liquor, and a muscle-bound neck-breaker who shattered people for coin.

The Man had just put the patients to sleep. The lights were out. The few nurses on staff were monitoring other things and he'd told them to give these folks a wide berth. They had some talking to do.

Steele reminded the Man of his debt: he'd taken out a loan to gamble with in his youth: money that had aided him in his pursuit to become a doctor, money that had helped build his inane hospice center in the middle of bumfuck nowhere, money that glistened from his gold watch down to the shine on his custom leather shoes.

He won that money and had not repaid his loan and in the time since, the amount to be paid back had grown exponentially.

Since this was a delicate matter, Steele had arrived in person to see that he be reimbursed and to make it known that no one successfully hid from him and lived.

The Man had one week to repay the debt owed.

The Man had heard stories about Steele through the years. Even before he found himself begging for a loan from him, he had carefully considered what kind of bed he was crawling into and just what bugs wriggled in the sheets.

Steele was a pseudonym: apparently back in the day, his face was plastered on multiple billboards, across the television, film, and media triumvirate. He made men envious to project the same presence and stamina; women melted and fantasized about being at his side (Janet highly doubted this—the Man insisted).

But when the lights faded and the cameras turned away, Steele did whatever Steele wanted and his associates: the witch, the trickster, and the neck-breaker were his collectors of secrets, of money, of whatever he desired.

Steele was the kind of man who didn't believe in

boundaries: who was always testing just how far the human spirit could be drawn before it would snap beneath him. He believed there was a heaven and a hell and that he was of celestial divinity, destined to walk among gilded roads while leering down at the squalor below. His sycophant cronies followed his every whim because they believed he could grant them eternity.

The stories of what happened to those who didn't pay back Steele were all as grandiose as the Man's claims of Steele's godliness were. People went missing in the night on their ways home from work; their bodies were found months later behind bricked up walls, anchored to cement blocks in the harbors, gorged on by rats in basements of abandoned factories, dropped from airplanes into forests to be speared by ancient conifers… Every one sounded more ridiculous than the last.

But there were hundreds of stories. Hundreds of legends floating in a mist that passed from seedy traveler to seedy traveler. Steele had become an urban legend.

His lieutenants had stories of their own that were somehow wilder and more unbelievable. Heads twisted clean off by the Neck-Breaker, bodies perforated like pincushions by the Trickster, fingernails wrenched off and eyeballs plucked by the Witch for her rituals… Some said the worst were left to Steele himself.

So, when all four of them showed up at the clinic and all four made the Man swear to pay the debt in a week's time, he took them damn well seriously.

He charged his clients' families more money at first. He lied to say that it was for extra security as things ratcheted up, as the world turned more violent, dried out, tried to chew and spit out humanity like gristle.

They paid. They *all* paid.

But it wasn't enough.

The Man asked them for all the money they could spare. He made sure to emphasize how lucky these families were that they'd found his clinic, to make sure they knew he and his staff would do anything to protect his patients and intimated how stingy they were if they couldn't commit more green for the people they loved. He said he remembered Janet's dad particularly: how withered he seemed when he delivered what he'd made from selling their house and their land.

The money was enough to satisfy the returned loan. But that wasn't enough to satisfy Steele. He wanted the Man to know never to borrow from him again. He was going to kill him. But the Man was already dying from cancer and he said as much, begging for whatever remained of his life.

Steele preferred the idea of a long, suffering death to a quick one. But the Man needed another blow, another reminder that would bleed in his memory, like being razed by shark's teeth.

Each one of his clinic patients was given a lethal dose before their night's sleep. Not one of them knew. Not one of them woke, including Amos.

The staff were executed en masse, bodies left to rot in the swimming pool.

Steele bid the man adieu and he and his companions left.

The Man, haunted by guilt, buried each and every patient before running to town, before building his ugly fortress of a home there, before eventually dying there.

Janet then asked the question she'd been meaning to ask: "What's in your precious folder?"

She'd looked months ago. Numbers. Names. She needed to understand.

"That's how much money I took from each patient's family," he blubbered. "I had hoped to pay it back someday. But…"

"But, what?"

"I realized there was no point. This world doesn't reward people for doing the right thing anymore. It just takes. And takes. And cuts. And bleeds."

When Janet retraced the numbers and the names later on and recognized her dad's name and what he'd given, a siege of sadness hit her. The numbers felt impossible. How could that much money be offered out of desperation, out of love and not be enough to satisfy one human being?

Janet's next question to the Man was steeped in venom: "Where is Steele?"

The Man, now rocking piteously back and forth in a spider-web-wrapped beetle's body had twitched. "You won't get anywhere near him. His lieutenants will cast you off faster than a lightning bolt on an iron rod. Forget it, girl. Let it go."

Janet set her jaw. "Where *the fuck* is he?"

"You are a stubborn little shit, aren't you? Stubborn and stupid and you're going to throw your life away because you think you're owed redemption? Have you not seen the world you live in? Redemption is for saps. The rest of us dropped our hubris and survived."

She cocked her head. "You didn't."

The Man gave a nervous chuckle. "No. I suppose not."

"Where is Steele?"

"The biggest place in Town," the Man answered, resignation coloring his tone. His voice shook as though he was enduring frozen temperatures. "The Hierophant Hotel. Penthouse floor."

Hotel. Janet sneered. Before everything fell to pieces, it used to be lovely. But ever since, it was always suffused in a sense of warning, of foreboding. Now, she knew why.

"That brings our conversation to an end," she said with no tone. She wasn't thankful it was over. She wasn't happy with anything she'd learned. If anything, it drove the nail down into her harder. She wanted Steele. She wanted to watch his blood slither down the sides of his face, wanted to look into his cold, dead eyes. Her skin was hot and pricked with the promise of revenge.

"In that case," The Man panted. "Leave me to die. I've had too much of this world."

Janet clicked her tongue.

The fox emerged from the shadows: pelt sifted in sparkling dust and rust-colored blood spatter. Its eyes tinged the warm color of red rock and hazed over mildly. Where once she'd listened to Amos's cheerful voice in a fox's presence, there was nothing but silence now. Hugh hadn't shared in his partner's general merriment. Hugh didn't give anything away at all.

The fox loped forward toward the last insect: wings plucked, buzzing meekly in the glass bowl, and promptly ate it.

The Man made no noise as his temporary body was devoured.

Janet stared at the empty bowl for a moment before she

stood and took in her derelict home for the last time. Then, they left for the hotel.

SEVEN

Janet remembered when the Hierophant Hotel first opened in Town. There was upheaval about it: its style clashed with the quiet, rural blush already situated. It was too grandiose, too opulent…and the locals thought it would bring trouble.

Perhaps Hierophant had been like a wolf in sheep's clothing trying to blend with the herd. It didn't exactly fit in and people regarded it either with fear or aberrant wonder. Maybe the gentrification that had swelled into other nearby towns had finally come for this one.

On a beautiful summer day, she'd gone with her parents to see it. Hugh had a business meeting there in one of the adjoining ballrooms, so she and Amos had an hour to probe its hallways, skirt the lobby, and ride its old-fashioned cage elevator up and down to every floor.

After the fall, the hotel immediately booted its tenants, boarded up its massive windows, and locked its doors. They didn't want to cater to the needy, she figured. After all, that crown-molding, gold-leafed and sculpted to perfection, must be kept intact. Couldn't have dirty interlopers sleeping on its cushy carpets or children's cries echo into the high ceilings of its lobby lest they soak in like ghosts. The riches were meant to be enjoyed only by the rich (or by anyone who corrupted their own morals to align with them).

She'd always assumed it had been the hotel staff who had closed it up but knowing it was this Steele character and his minions made so much more sense. But why had he stayed in Town at all? Why hadn't he left, returned to the spoils of whatever grandeur awaited him back where he'd come from?

There was either something here he wanted or something had forced him to stay. As much as Janet wanted to know which one, she was certain no one else in town knew or would tell her. All she had was the exhaustive diatribe that the Man had given her.

In the nighttime, when Janet approached Town, she could see the hotel's lights glowing high above the houses and the paleness of the streetlights.

The heat of summer made this Town almost unlivable now. Much like the splintering apart of the outskirts, townsfolk had gathered up their many suitcases stuffed full of too short shorts, crop tops and racer-backs, badminton sets, croquet wickets, mallets, and balls…inflatable swim animals… They'd all get stuffed into cars and they'd venture northwest in search of water where it was still said to be in dwindling ponds once called the Great Lakes.

They'd left the town sparse: the only lingering bodies those who had stolen their wealth and hadn't the faintest idea what to do with it. They'd drink whole wine collections away while locking themselves in home theaters to rewatch their favorite films again and again—to pretend that the world outside was the same as they'd left it.

Nighttime was temperate: the low hundreds of the day quelling into the low eighties, the wind swirling in over her shoulders and mixing in her hair.

Janet surveyed the streets for movement and finding none, made her approach on the hotel.

Dim lights shone through the glass in the floors above. Someone was home. Someone was waiting.

She glanced behind her at the fox. It stared at the door, or at least she thought it did. It was hard to tell exactly where it fixed its gaze through the red clouding of its pupils.

"Are you ready, Hugh?"

There was no reply.

Janet gripped the door handle and turned it.

She hadn't expected it to open. It didn't make sense that it should. All the windows on the first floor were boarded up, the siding chipped and sand-blasted. No one had visibly set foot in it for almost a decade, or at least, that was the rumor.

But it opened.

Goosebumps bristled on Janet's arms as she pushed in to the dark lobby. Even in shadow, its luxury was a sight to behold. Her boots echoed softly through the vast room as she stepped further into it.

A crystal chandelier hung over a set of armchairs before the stone-cold fireplace. The front desk was small and tucked in a corner with a giant grid of wooden boxes covering the wall behind it. Forgotten letters and packages still poked out of several slots.

The elevator sat quiet in the opposite corner of the lobby next to the entrance of the dining room. Flickering candlelight from within the small bar next door beckoned to her and Janet stilled.

If one of Steele's lackeys was down here, they'd have heard the front door open. They'd know she was there. The element of surprise was gone.

Janet's fingers smoothed over the head of the wrench on her belt as she cautiously approached the left side of the lobby and tried to look into the bar from a distance.

It was a tiny room, barely the size of her bedroom back home, with only two booths inside and a short bar-top with lacquered wood as smooth as glass. Someone sat on the stool in the back of the room, a black cowboy hat pulled low over his head.

He began to whistle. It was clear and crisp and practically cut the air with each precise note.

A man. Too lean to be the so-called Neck Breaker and obviously not the witch. Was this Steele himself?

What was that song? She recognized it and it hitched in her stomach when she finally pieced it together. It was her and her father's song: the one they danced to and they sang together before bedtime. The one that she had made Amos remember himself with months ago after she'd brought him back…

How did he know? How did this fuck *know*?

That's when he looked up: the face seemingly uncurling from beneath the hat. His smile: that eerie smile seemed to overtake his whole goddamned face.

Trickster.

The Man said it was like the Trickster found a back door into your head. The kind you made when you were a kid and you were afraid of getting locked in all by yourself so you created a way for a friend or a loved one to get through to you. Hers had been buried, covered by thick tendrils of ivy and moss, left to rot this whole time as the years passed.

But the bastard got in.

The Man said the bastard somehow *always* got in no matter who his mark was.

"What's the matter?" The Trickster called, the pitch of his voice flittering almost in time with the candle. "Don't you want to sing it with me, Ella?"

Goosebumps rippled over Janet's arms.

How? How did he know? How had he guessed her real name unless…

"Did you kill him?" The words snaked out between her gnashing teeth, the rumble of anger like a barreling wind through grass. The fox, Amos, Hugh… she wasn't even sure who she meant. Maybe all of them.

The Trickster just smiled. The candlelight made it seem like his face had contorted to try and contain that smile and it was bowing out, losing its shape…

"Did you fucking touch him?" She slid the wrench from her belt.

"What are you gonna do, little girl?" he purred. One boot touched the floor beside his stool as he half-stood.

Her fingers squeezed the metal and it warmed against her palm. "Break your fucking smile."

The Trickster giggled and blew out the candle.

EIGHT

"What are you making there, sweetheart?" Amos's voice floated in from somewhere nearby. The air smelled sweet, like fresh strawberries. He'd been cutting them over the sink in the kitchen while she sat at the dining room table, her legs swinging. Music was on, it was always on in the background. Possibly Fleetwood Mac; that was one of her father's favorites.

"It's the night sky!" she said excitedly, holding up the paper. She'd scrawled a turquoise green lawn with her crayons, scribbled navy across the top of the sheet and was in the midst of sticking glittering stars to the paper with white glue. As she lifted the drawing for him to see, a couple stars slid back down onto the table.

"Wow!" He dropped into the chair next to her, smirking as he took her drawing in his hands. "It's so lifelike! I feel like I'm right there!"

"I was going to put a moon, but I forgot to leave space for it…" she said, hanging her head a little.

He put the paper back down on the table. "That's okay. You still can! Here, gimme the glue."

She handed it over.

"Where do you want it? Here?" He pointed to the left top corner. "Or here?" He moved to the right.

"Yeah, right there!" She giggled.

Tipping the bottle upside down, Amos outlined a circle and then filled it in with the glue. It gleamed white under the sunlight sifting in through the small window over the sink.

"There. Now, just wait for it to dry, and you'll have your moon." He leaned in and kissed her forehead.

She smiled until she noticed a streak of red fingerprint in her grass. "Aw, no!"

Ella watched Amos's grin as it vanished, as lines appeared in his forehead. "Uh oh. Dang strawberries. Really thought I washed my hands. I'm sorry, honey."

Had he known then? Did he have an inkling of what was going to happen to him? She couldn't recall.

"It's okay," she whispered. She grabbed her black pencil and drew around it: gave it a body, legs, a head and a long tail. "It's a fox now!"

Amos blinked. Had there been a glimmer of a tear? "That's my girl. Such a creative problem-solver."

Janet moved first. She was never the kind to wait for the other person to make the first attack, never the kind to allow them momentum or opportunity. But the Trickster had clearly expected her arrival and had been waiting for some time.

So, she didn't run into the bar. Instead, Janet took off into the restaurant beside it and immediately searched for cover. There were a number of white cloth-covered tables in the area along with two buffets and the doors to the kitchen off to the right side of the room.

The kitchen would afford her more weapons but likely fewer places to hide and the probability of him finding her beneath a table was lower. All she needed was the element of surprise.

So, she chose a table toward the back of the room and ducked under it. In the darkness, her heartbeat thundered in her own head. Her fingers grazed over the items of her tool belt until she found the one she needed: the spray bottle.

She waited.

It was several moments before she heard soft, even footfalls on the carpet in the restaurant doorway. Then, the Trickster's whistle. "Playing games, are we?" He cackled. "I do love a good game."

The overhead lights suddenly came on.

"Where, oh, where could you be?"

Janet couldn't see through the table cloth which she was thankful for because that meant he couldn't see her either. She heard the whoosh of a nearby cloth being thrown.

"Were you good at hide and seek, Ella?" the Trickster asked, his voice far too close for her liking. "Did you play to win or just hide from the others?"

She'd never played hide and seek with other children; only her parents. The kids at school had been cautious—no—not cautious; exclusive. They knew who their friends were and she wasn't one of them. Plus, they'd heard stories about the weird girl and her two dads who lived outside of Town.

When she tried to do the things they did, they'd move

away from her, or even tell her she couldn't sit with them, or use their colored pencils, or that she didn't understand what they were conversing about.

The whorl of another tablecloth slammed Janet back into her body. Fuck. She'd gotten caught up. He'd gotten in her mind again. She shook her head, blinked. *Stay in fucking control,* she urged herself.

"Not there either!" the Trickster's voice tittered. "You're good at this! But you've been hiding for a really long time, haven't you?" His shadow grew on the other side of the tablecloth. "Got your nerve up a couple months ago. We were watching. We could see evvverythiiiing…"

Janet stiffened. The hotel was visible from most parts of town. If they'd been on a top floor: they actually might have seen her and her attempt on the Man's life.

"It was going to be quite a show." His voice lowered to a growl as he said, "Too bad you chickened out."

She had. Janet squeezed the bottle as she thought about that night. What an absolute clusterfuck.

Stay in control!

"You let down dear daddy! How pathetic!"

Heat clustered in Janet's cheeks and forehead. She exhaled through her nose and closed her eyes for a moment.

Stay in—

Boots slammed on the table above her and she barely held back a gasp.

"Poor sad Ella," he exclaimed from overhead. "Too weak to do anything. To afraid to go the extra mile and put that man in the ground. The man who let your muddled, feeble waste of a father get put down like an animal!"

Janet bit her gums to keep from making any noise, even as it became harder to take any breaths, even as her every thought erupted in rage, rage, *fucking rage…*

The table creaked and shifted and an oval shadow appeared down over the side, silhouetted by the cloth.

"I…see…you…"

Janet fell onto her back, screaming. Her boots slammed up into the bottom of the table as she kicked as hard as she could.

The table's weight shifted and toppled, spilling the Trickster onto the carpet.

Scrambling to her feet, Janet hastened around the downed furniture, bottled squeezed in her hand as she leapt on him. Her wrench hand swung first, capping him across the cheek.

Teeth crunched under its blow as the Trickster's laugh was cut short. It built into a snarl and he shoved her off him with a wave of his arm before going for something in his jacket pocket.

The room spun as she spilled onto her stomach. Janet flipped herself in time for his arm to extend. Her left shoulder detonated in hot pain and she fell back. A dart. A throwing dart in her shoulder…

Moments later, his weight dropped on her, prying the wrench from her hand. The Trickster squealed and laughed and cried as he gazed into her eyes. "Broke my…umph… fuck….you!"

She hadn't noticed how green his eyes were before. Weirdly light green. His hand ripped the dart out of her shoulder and slammed it back down into it.

New fire erupted and Janet howled as his arm went up

and down like a lever: driving the dart deeper; her shoulder burning, screaming…

Janet swung the bottle up and squeezed the trigger over and over, the pressure beneath her finger steady. Streams of liquid splashed against the Trickster's face: his cheeks, his eyes, up his nose… It was only a second before his juddering hand let go of the dart and flew up to protect his face.

He screeched: a sound she hadn't heard since she was a child. Like the errant cries of gulls when they'd visited the beach, back when the ocean was only a half an hour drive from them and not a three to four hour one. High-pitched and blubbered and mewling all together.

Janet huffed, her shoulder muscles throbbing. Letting go of the bottle, she tipped onto her uninjured side and propped herself up into a sitting position. Blood smeared across her clothing and down her side, more blooming by the second. She watched as the Trickster squirmed on the floor and wildly wiped at his face.

"Hurts like a bitch, doesn't it?" she asked. "I figured that any fuck who killed my parents didn't deserve to just die, you know. He had to suffer. He had to wish he was dead."

She got to her feet. The room pitched and she caught herself on the buffet, hand clawing at one of the cloth napkins there. She pushed it against her shoulder and gritted her teeth against the pain.

"Glue is a great binder as it turns out. Watered down with some rubbing alcohol, it makes a nice spray consistency and obviously sticks to everything. Do you know what urushiol is? It's fine: I get it if you can't answer. Probably burns like hell. It's the oil that coats the leaves of poison ivy. No matter how dry it gets out there, that stuff seems to run rampant, especially around my place.

"It was pretty easy to mash up and add to this bottle. I guess that could have been enough, but I thought, why not shoot for the stars? After all, it's what my—what did you call him?—muddled, feeble waste of a father taught me. So, I added stinging nettle, too."

The Trickster staggered to his feet. He ran and slammed straight into the wall a few feet in front of her. When he hit the ground, he immediately vomited.

"All that swiping at your eyes probably made those little needles spread around, inject all their chemicals into your face. Bet it feels extra nice in that open jaw wound."

He panted, strings of saliva hanging from his open mouth as he pushed himself up on all fours. His face was a sickening red color: red from the rash spreading over his skin, the exertion, the sickness…

Janet retrieved her wrench from the ground where the Trickster had knocked it away and stood over him. "I'll end it quickly if you answer my question: did you kill him?"

The Trickster spat up more bile. "N-n-no! W-wasn't me!"

"Who?" When he didn't answer, Janet touched the side of his head with the wrench head. "Tell me!"

"Witch! Witch did…" His tongue dragged against his teeth and his words devolved into anguished moans again.

"Great. Let's keep this moving then." Janet swung back to hit him.

He launched himself toward her and she barely had a moment to dodge as he sprawled across the ground, screaming.

"Suppose I should have expected that," she said to herself. Standing over him, both legs on either side, she brought the wrench down on the back of his skull: once, twice (there was a crack), three times and something gave.

A weird whine leaked out of his throat and dissipated into silence.

Letting the wrench drop against the carpet, Janet staggered to the nearest chair at a table and slumped into it. Fireworks went off in her shoulder: banging and fizzling and searing. She needed to patch the wounds, stop the pain...

She glanced out the door toward the lobby and clicked her tongue. After a moment of waiting, she clicked again.

The fox appeared around the corner and padded toward her.

"Stand still, Hugh," she said, reaching up to his neck. In the collar there, she slid free a small pouch filled with pills and a tinier one with pulverized herbs. She swallowed three of the pills immediately.

Finding a serrated knife on the buffet, she cut part of her shirt away to expose the four puncture wounds there. They were already purple and smeared in blood, the skin raised. When she touched them, each one felt like a match being stuck inside.

Pinching a small bit of the herb between her fingers, she pushed it against the puncture wounds. More blood oozed under the pressure from her finger and her stomach flipped with the desire to puke.

Aster: it would help with the pain. Wiping her finger on the seat, she wrapped the bag up and tucked it back into the fox's collar.

The ruckus that had occurred should have brought others out. She'd half expected to be ambushed as she sat there in the restaurant attending to her wounds. But the others didn't appear. No one was going to check in with the Trickster. They knew he'd failed.

Now, she'd have to go in search of the rest of them.

Janet stood. She wiped down the head of her wrench before replacing it in her belt. Then, she returned to the lobby and climbed the stairs for the next floor.

NINE

Something was wrong with Hugh. It was clear to Janet by his silence and by his disregard for her entire battle with the Trickster. Where Amos in the fox's body would have come running to defend her months ago, Hugh had stood waiting in the lobby, listening to her get stabbed multiple times.

Only when she'd clicked her tongue had he trotted into the room.

She'd been afraid to talk with him at first. Memories of her dad were ones she'd submerged deeply. Amos's death was a blow that had scarred them both. Hugh's was one that woke her in the dead of night, clawing at whatever she'd found for a blanket, choking on tears.

Visions of his emaciated body discarded along the train tracks stained her mind. She'd only found pieces of him to bring home and couldn't discard the horrible thought of the train dragging his body beneath its shuddering carriages toward its next eventual stop.

Surely, he wouldn't remember how he died. How much would he though? Would he remember them wandering the edges of town aimlessly while they starved? Would he remember how he'd cried in the darkness about Amos whenever he thought she was asleep? Would he remember even losing Amos to his worsening condition?

Maybe it was best to start slow. Back from the beginning. She hadn't done this with Amos. She'd gone for full anonymity. With Hugh, she was sure he would fight with her, that he didn't need convincing. All she had to do was catch him back up to speed.

So, she started with early memories.

Where Amos had always encouraged her growth of knowledge and understanding the world around her, Hugh was her dream weaver. He whisked her away to their backyard for adventure after adventure. Sometimes, they'd lose themselves in the woods following a game trail for miles; sometimes they'd lay on the lawn and study the clouds overhead, save dragonflies from the greenhouse before they expired, count the eggs in whatever birds' nests they could find…

Appreciation of nature was Hugh's catalyst in nearly every lesson of the things he taught her after they started homeschooling her. He wanted her to understand its power, value its gifts and curses, and acknowledge its ability to absorb and obliterate.

He was the first one to really start explaining their magic to her. Week after week, as they hiked or as they gardened, he'd describe the various herbs and weeds and flowers. They'd pluck samples to brew into teas, crush into powders, and macerate into pastes.

Slowly, he told her how to use them to conjure.

"Okay," he'd said, as he'd picked up a rock from the

ground. "Say you wanted to throw this rock. You have your hand, you have the rock and what you need is motion to get it from here to there. Words are your propulsion to make your spell move. Otherwise, it's just you and the mixture."

She wasn't sure she'd understood at first but the fact that words were important was ingrained in her. She just had to find out exactly which words.

She'd retold the story to Hugh as the fox had lain on the bed panting and staring at her with those clouded red eyes.

Nothing. Not a flicker of recognition. Not a word.

But he'd responded to the clicks. He responded to the name "Hugh"…or at least, she thought he had after the fact. She'd had to substitute ingredients and she knew after the many times she'd brought Amos back that just the wrong amount would affect *how* he came back.

Had using spit instead of tears made him mute? Had it made him apathetic?

Janet opened her eyes. She had stopped only on the third step of the stairs to the second floor, intending to listen for any noise that might signal an attack from above. Her thoughts had run away with her again, or maybe it was her mind's trick to distract her from the agony in her shoulder.

The pain sharpened. She choked down a grunt as she continued to climb.

Paintings of churning seas and ships with full sails lorded over the staircase landing as she reached it. The rich wood behind it was carved in swirls and eddies much like the waves in a storm. They curled into the shapes of leaves and flowers as they stretched away from the corners and blended into the dark red wallpaper that took over for the bare accents downstairs.

The stairs turned one hundred and eighty degrees as Janet followed them to the second floor. A long hallway stretched to her left and right lined with doorways that all looked exactly alike. She reasoned that anyone staying on this floor must have heard the commotion downstairs and would be lying in wait of her.

"Eeny, meenie, miny, mo..." she whispered before deciding left.

The doors were closed, the tell-tale gold number marking each one just above the peep-holes. Only five were on each side of her, the hall bisecting them into twos with one room lingering at the end of each hall. The hotel was tall and commanded a presence for sure, but the rooms were large and the entire hotel was only home to sixteen in total, including the penthouse on the top floor.

While she'd never been inside of any of the suites, her younger self had pictured enormous accommodations: multiple luxurious rooms for guests to fan out their belongings, hot tubs to languish in, king-sized beds for them to burrow into and dream days away in.

As Janet approached the first room, the fox standing behind her without sound, she detected a sweetness on the air. It reminded her of wildflowers, of honey and afternoons spent playing tea party out by the greenhouse with her stuffed animals.

The thought prickled as she turned her attention away from the door and down to the opposite end of the hall: to the figure who stood poised at the end.

Long flowing smoke gray linens clung to the woman's

pale arms and sheathed her willowy figure as she stared daggers. Her eyes were rubbed with black powder and seemed like two white stones thrown into shadow. Her white-blonde tresses seemed suspended, as if riding an invisible current all around her.

Janet went rigid, her hand finding the handle of her wrench. But even as she started to lift it, a heaviness draped over her. She stumbled into the door beside her and it creaked in beneath her weight. She dropped onto the carpet inside, brain skittering like a mouse trapped in a corner.

Why couldn't she *move*? Why couldn't she *think*?

She tried to slide the wrench from its pocket on her belt, the scent of the wildflowers blossoming stronger, infecting everything.

"Fuck," she murmured, her head lolling. It felt a thousand pounds heavier. Every bit of her was glued to the floor.

The Witch stepped into view overhead, upside-down on the floor-ceiling, no smile on her face, no light in her black and white eyes. She knelt down and Janet felt fingernails scrape delicately at her scalp as her eyes closed.

"Shh. Dream, girl. Dream of the flowers."

TEN

Janet dreamed of asters, of teardrops, and stars born from them as they struck the night sky. In the haze of imagery that had overtaken her consciousness, a new pain needled through it: harsh, like a buzz saw spinning against her skin, shredding flesh.

In the ocean of hurt, she saw Hugh: the way she remembered him most often. "Think of asters," he softly told her. "Think of the Greek goddess, Astraea, from our story-times. It's okay to be sad. Every teardrop becomes a star, sweetheart."

Her throat thickened as she sobbed. "But I don't want him to go! I don't want him to!"

His face pinched for a moment as he reached forward and held her to him. She smelled wildflowers. "It'll just be for a little bit," he said, voice cracking. "But Amos is always going to be here." She felt his finger gently stroke her head. "And every time you sing your song, he'll know it's you, okay?"

"You promise?"

"I do."

He couldn't promise that. He shouldn't have promised that.

Burning.

Searing.

Tearing.

Janet's eyes opened and blurry smoke swam in them. As her awareness spread, so did the pain: rising, spreading, raging until... She screamed, scrunched her eyes tighter and opened them again.

The soft glow of lights swelled in the space around her, glinting off the full-length mirror opposite her, gleaming on every polished wood surface. Her reflection sliced through the confusion: tied to a straight-backed chair, clothing bloodied and torn.

Behind her, the Witch wrenched a set of pliers back from the chair and Janet's entire world was consumed by agony as she doubled over and howled.

"You back yet, little one?" The Witch leered, her voice buttery smooth. It reminded Janet of the receptionist's voice from the clinic where they'd taken Amos. The kind of voice who read the books on tape she liked. Trusting, gentle-seeming...

"Expected more of a fight from you," she said, her smile white; perfect in the reflection. "They said you knew your spells, that you were skilled." She shook her head. "You didn't even check for a basic headcase spell. You blundered right through it when you crossed the front door downstairs."

Janet grunted. It explained why she couldn't get out of her own thoughts with the Trickster...why he was just waiting for her...

"I'll admit, most people are totally overcome in a matter of minutes but it took longer with you. Must be all that training your daddies gave you." She held up a tiny bloodied rectangle with the pliers. "Means your nails are worth something to me."

Janet's fingers shrieked behind her back. She gnashed her teeth together as she searched the room for something, anything she could use to her advantage and—oh—her mind chirped with hope… The fox stood in the open doorway watching.

She clicked her tongue.

It didn't move.

She tried again.

The fox was motionless but still just…watching.

"You're greener than I thought," the Witch sighed behind her. "It's not your pet, you realize? I'm not even sure if it knows where it is…what it is…"

"Hugh," Janet called to the fox.

Blank. Not even a flutter of eyelids or flick of fur rising.

"Oh dear." The Witch clucked. "How embarrassing. Not only can't you command it, you can't even tell what's inside…"

A feeling broiled deep in Janet's stomach with the words. She stared at the fox, at the vacancy in its eyes, at the red. "Hugh!" she cried.

"You silly little bitch." The Witch's tone was dismissive. Janet watched her blonde hair quake side to side as she shook her head. "You're that naïve that you thought that was your dad?" Her giggle rippled like water though the air until it turned harsh. "Darling, I don't know what thing you managed to clutch hold of and shove into the body of that animal, but it definitely isn't Hugh."

Something about the way she said her dad's name made

the air in Janet's lungs turn stale. No. She was imagining it. This was all apart of the witch's trick to keep her down, keep her from getting free.

The Witch clicked her tongue.

The fox loped further into the room. A thin string of drool fell from the corner of its mouth to the rug.

"Poor soul has probably been part of the earth longer than you've been alive," the Witch said. Snapping her fingers, the fox staggered over to her, the ends of its fur brushing against Janet's leg.

"There, there," the witch cooed as she stroked the fox's head. "It'll all be over soon."

Janet eyed the collar and the various pouches of herbs there. Her hand strained trying to reach but hard plastic cut into her wrists.

"And what's this?" The Witch fingered the pouches on the collar. "Some homemade spells? So cute." Plucking a couple bags from the panting fox's collar, she opened her hand and poured the contents out.

Janet's attention peaked. Corydalis powder. Its golden color popped against the Witch's skin.

"Hmm. Rustic."

"Remedies," Janet coughed. "Things to numb the pain if I needed." Or to cause it.

"I'll tell you what." The Witch grinned. "I'll even let you have some. It'll numb your fingers while I work on your eyes."

The Witch overturned the pouch and the particles tinkled over Janet's skin and stuck to the blood on her fingers.

Janet's lips cracked into a small smile. "You silly little bitch," she whispered back and flicked her fingers out. The veins across her hands and up her arms bulged. Every breath that coursed over her tongue felt like she was breathing in fire and when she let it go, the air around her split.

One moment, the Witch was right behind her. The next: her body hurtled over the giant bed behind them and cracked into the wall above the headboard.

The fox collapsed against the plaster next to the wardrobe on her left and the chair beneath Janet crumbled. A deep crevice splintered along the floor and shattered a nearby window.

Words. Her dad was right about them mattering. Especially ones used to make her feel small. She could flip them around like a flaming baton in a talent show.

The plastic around Janet's wrists snapped and its brittle pieces dropped to the rug as she leapt to her feet. Running to the nightstand, she grabbed the wrench from her tool belt and vaulted onto the bed where the witch was just turning over.

One hand clawed out in the air before her, the Witch flicked her wrist.

Janet's legs swept out from underneath her. She slammed against the carpet, seething as her fingers throbbed and her shoulder ignited.

She lobbed the wrench at the witch.

Its handle spun wildly until it crunched against the latter's head. The Witch slumped on the mattress.

Janet regained her composure, her feet aching as she snatched up the pouch from where the witch dropped it and pinched another handful of corydalis from inside it.

Just as the Witch raised her head, Janet inhaled and blew

the herbs into her assailant's face before she huffed, "You. Silly. Little. Bitch!"

The air vibrated. The particles become needles, pins that shot into the perfect skin of the Witch's face: into her high cheekbones, her glowing skin, her soft eyes…

Those holes split, opening up a yawning cavern from the tip of her forehead down through her top lip.

The bellow that loosed from the blonde Witch was that of a banshee: a wailing that echoed from deep in the woods in her childhood, wailing that had brought both her father's into her room to stand guard over her windows at night.

There were things that lived in the darkness that even they wouldn't tell her about: things she had gone looking for eventually, things that had hardened her resolve, that had driven her dad's lessons about magic home.

But that scream…it rippled the still water in her mind. It reminded her of when she was afraid and had someone to protect her. Everything inside her clenched with hatred at feeling that helplessness again.

Snatching the wrench from the soft down of the duvet, Janet straddled the crumpled conjurer, her nail-less fingers groping for a hunk of her enemy's wild hair. She gazed down into the mess that was left of her face. "Did you kill him?!"

The Witch sputtered from the mouth that went horizontal while the one now etched vertically through her skull seeped gore over the contours of her white eyes and the furrows where her nose once was.

Janet wrenched the hair higher until the Witch's trembling head lifted from the sheets. She repeated her question.

The tiniest, barest nod of her sharp chin. The Witch swallowed and spoke in faint gasps, "Poison. I made it. I visited each patient personally and—"She swallowed again. "—watched them go cold as the nurses delivered it."

"And the fox?"

Silence turned to a throaty gurgle of laughter.

Janet's fingers sunk into the Witch's skull as her grip went deeper. "Did you kill my fox?"

Blood burbled up from the Witch's vertical mouth. "As-ask the neck-breaker."

Shoving the Witch's head back against the mattress, Janet buried the wrench in her face with a slick crunch.

ELEVEN

Janet lay on the bed staring up at the blood-spattered ceiling. Pain engulfed her hands, threading up her fingers to her palms. She didn't want to look at them. To acknowledge the injuries would be to add new torment to them, just like when she was a child.

Running along in the woods, she'd get scraped up by all manner of broken sticks and thorns without noticing. Only when her parents reacted did she finally see and the pain slipped in like a silent passenger along with panic.

She sat up and climbed off the bed, her gaze following the cracks in the hotel walls to the broken window where the wind rushed in to tickle the curtains. Finally, her sights settled on the fox in a heap across the room. Janet walked to it and knelt beside its no longer rising and falling chest, saw the clarity of its eyes no longer clouded in red.

A tear slid from her eye down along her nose. It was never Hugh. She still hadn't been able to bring him back, no matter what she'd learned. No matter what she had thought she'd learned.

She ran the back of her hand along the tuft of fur on

its cheek and closed her eyes in apology. Then, unclasping its collar, she tucked the remaining pouches of herbs in her jacket pocket and let the leather drop onto the carpet.

No more games, she thought. *Two down and two more to go.*

Standing, Janet reclaimed her wrench and left the room. The hall outside was empty. She locked her sights on the floor above and returned to the stairs. Somewhere, high above, the steady rippling of a piano called down to her.

As Janet climbed, she seethed with thoughts of home, of the last time she'd heard her dad play his piano. The heartbroken look in his eye when they had to leave all of their beautiful things behind. They couldn't take everything with them.

That piano had sat in the middle of their dining room for another seven years: dust-coated, autumn leaves blown in around its legs, the sun still playing over its smooth brown top. She'd tried to play it once and it had ended with her sobbing in the room that used to be hers until she fell asleep.

The sound of that piano now made the tears blur in her eyes anew and made the fury burn hotter.

Her steady steps turned to blundering. All she needed was a room alone with Steele, room for her to use every single tool on her belt to make sure he suffered. All she needed was—

A hand gripped the front of her jacket and yanked her off her feet.

Janet yelped as the floor rushed up to greet her and she toppled across it. Shoulder screaming, she barely had a moment to flip over before iron fingers closed on her arms and hefted her from the floor.

The behemoth neck-breaker in front of her brought every imagining of the word "giant" to her head. As he lifted her nearly four feet from the ground, she stared down into his gnarled face, a slab of a forehead and beady eyes crushed between two doughy cheeks.

He casually tossed her back into the nearest wall and she broke against it before buckling on the floor. Every joint ached and her anxiety spiraled as she groped for something on her tool belt to defend herself with.

Finding the flathead screw driver, she leapt to her feet, rose the implement up over her head and drove it down toward the giant's chest.

A meaty hand caught her wrist as it came foreword and another snatched it out of her hand. She heard it bang against something glass down the hall as she was once again lifted into the air, this time by one arm.

Pinwheeling her legs, she kicked the giant in his soft belly and he bowed in response, dropping her.

Landing on her tailbone, Janet scooched backward as he slammed a fist down, nearly catching her.

Janet seized the next tool out of her belt as another fist came down at her. She batted it away with her hammer deftly before blocking another attack.

The great hand latched onto the hammer head and tore it out of her grip.

Fuck. She was losing tool after tool left and right. Janet went for the pouch of corydalis in her pocket and barely had it out before the fist reached her face.

The world exploded. Janet dropped against the carpet,

the powder lost from her grip. A high-pitched whine reeled through her head. She inhaled and her entire nose flared with pain.

Blood rolling down into her lips, thick fingers clutched around her throat and ripped her up from the ground. Her entire body dangled like a lead weight beneath her as his palm squished against her trachea. She scrabbled at his hand, struggling to breathe.

He glared into her as if she were a mere insect, as if he were her a few hours ago with the Man in the bowl and squeezed her harder.

Twinkling stars flooded her vision and her hearing dropped out, overtaken by the overwhelming drumbeat of her own heart slamming in her temples. She wheezed, trying to say something, anything.

Then, she was airborne. The hall floor thundered up to greet her. Warm air launched down her throat. She sucked it in, savoring each breath.

The Neck-Breaker had toppled forward and barely caught himself on his hands and knees. As he got back up, he turned around.

Janet's followed his gaze, her brow puckering.

The Undertaker stood at the top of the stairs, his well-muscled arms hefting his metal shovel.

Growling, the Neck-Breaker launched at him.

The Undertaker took the hit and the two of them battered into the banister, wood cracking. He raised the shovel up and drove its handle into the Neck-Breaker's back once, twice before the brute dropped.

The Neck-Breaker swung an arm into the back of the

Undertaker's legs and he went down.

Janet held her throat as she watched, her other hand blindly searching her belt for a weapon.

The Neck-Breaker lay fist after fist after fist over the Undertaker, who's shovel had fallen to the side.

Janet slipped her Phillip's head screwdriver free and flung it as hard as she could. The handle struck the Neck-Breaker against his skull and made him stumble, enough to give the Undertaker a chance to grab his shovel, enough to allow him to drive the spear of the blade into the Neck-Breaker's side like a shish-kebab.

Blood fanned out, splurging over the floor and across the Undertaker as he pried his tool loose and went for a second strike.

The Neck-Breaker clocked him in the teeth with such force that it made the Undertaker sway before he toppled. The giant stumbled and plastered his hands over the gaping wound in his side.

Janet sprang into action and retrieving the dropped shovel, scooped up toward the bleeding slice. It slid in like an ice cream scoop through vanilla.

Janet put all her weight in the other end of the shovel and felt the flesh tear, hot blood lashing over her before the back of a hand whapped her in the cheek. She stumbled over the Undertaker as he struggled to get up and landed on her injured shoulder.

The world was spinning. Janet forced her palms into the floor, trying to blink away the banging in her skull and in every little muscle.

The Neck-Breaker plucked the shovel from his side as if

it was a thorn and plopped it down on the ground.

He…just…wouldn't…die.

Janet stood and stared at the hulking monster in front of her. "You killed my fox, you fucking asshole."

Blood spilling down the side of his shirt, down his pants and over his leather boots, the Neck-Breaker grinned.

She opened her arms out as wide as they could go. "Come and get me, you big fuck."

Opening his mouth into a vicious roar, the Neck-Breaker charged, his whole frame a locomotive as it careened toward her.

Janet held her breath, muscles straining.

The Undertaker shoved her out of the way.

Janet folded under his immense strength like a card table, clapping against the floor. Her cheek smacked into the wood, jaw banging as a warm darkness threatened to overtake her.

Behind her, the crack of wood reverberated through the stairwell along with the fading grunts of two leviathans. Far below, something clanged against metal and then the BOOM of a solid mass slammed into the lobby floor.

She lay there in a daze, studying the motes of dust as they floated in the dim lights around her. *Don't move*, she wanted to convince herself. *It's better if you don't.*

Eventually, her vision strayed to the broken banister. Her thoughts caught up and they pushed her body into motion. Descending the stairs was propelled by adrenaline, even when her body protested.

She saw the rumples of fabric against the stark white carpet in the lobby: the outline of a hand bent in an angle too strange for the arm it was connected to. Blood was spilled like an abstract painting. Atop slips and skewing arcs lay two bodies tangled in each other.

By the time she made it to the bottom, Janet was huffing in breaths and her throat threatened to ignite.

The Neck-Breaker was like a squashed fly: innards slipped from the hole in his side, arms mangled and elbows crushed and his face a blood smeared crater in the rug with his head twisted very much the wrong way.

The Undertaker hadn't fared much better. His legs were mangled, one up underneath him while his chest shallowly rose and fell. He gazed up at the ceiling, hazel eyes fluttering.

Janet knelt beside him.

She thought of a day where she was not strong and sorrow had her pinned to the floor: a day where parts of her dad lay scattered in the backyard because she didn't have the energy to bury them.

The Undertaker showed up at her home. Someone had sent him from town; she never found out who. He'd picked up her weakened body and put her in her old bed, even pulled the blankets up over her.

Then, he'd found the tree at the edge of the woods and laid her dad to rest there. He didn't leave a note. He didn't let her know when the job was done; he simply retreated back to town as if he were a child being called home before supper.

As Janet thought about that day, her ragged fingers crept over the Undertaker's bruised and dirtied knuckles. She held his hand as his breaths became fainter.

Maybe no one had sent him. Maybe he had heard the news of her dad's death from other vagrants. Maybe he had just come by himself out of kindness like he had done today.

Maybe kindness had nothing to do with it and it was all about what she had promised: that she was going to finish it. That she was going to upend the current status quo. Maybe he was just here to make sure she got the job done.

No matter what the reason, she whispered, "Thanks, buddy." When he didn't take another breath, and everything about him stopped moving, Janet closed her eyes and clenched her hands into fists.

Penthouse floor, here we come.

TWELVE

The stairs were much harder to climb a second time. While adrenaline had floated her down them, its presence was faltering. Everything hurt and the varieties of that hurt ranged from tingling to the feeling of being smashed with a cast iron frying pan over and over.

But there was only one left: Steele, the man himself. The one who had wrought so much pain to so many people for decades.

As Janet summited to the penthouse floor, she surveyed her nearly empty tool belt save for a pouch of herbs and her father's wrench: bloodied and scratched. She checked the pouch: only the Aster remained. She dipped her finger in, letting the particles stick to her and then pressed it into her various scrapes, against the soft meat of her fingers where her nails used to be, and even against the outside of her nose, which had swollen immensely.

It was a marginal difference: like trying to contain a bullet with a closed hand around the barrel. But eventually, the numbness came and she reclaimed a portion of her thoughts and focus back.

If the rest of the hotel had been lavish, the Penthouse floor was exquisite. Its wallpaper had resumed the white pristineness of the lobby, the swirls in the plaster gaining more filigree, the paintings leaving the oceans and dipping into landscapes of fields spotted with summer poppies and struck with lupine.

The piano music swelled from behind the closed door and ratcheted up Janet's resolve again. If she never heard the piano play again, she'd be fine. Pulling her wrench, Janet curled her hand around the ornate knob on the door, inhaled, and yanked it down.

The room spilled forward like a chasm of wealth and grandeur. A high ceiling tumbled toward the far wall where a sea of glass overlooked the miserable rambling Town below. This main room was dotted with plush accent chairs, a bar cart stocked to the brim with various bottles of alcohol and the oriental rug, lush to the point where her boots practically sank into it.

The piano sitting in the center of the room was unlike the one they had at home: a Steinway. It might have gleamed once if it wasn't so covered in dust. It was the kind of piano that belonged in a concert hall somewhere a hundred miles from here, best enjoyed with the acoustics of a huge stage and a much broader room than this to fully appreciate its sound.

Sitting at it was a tall, broad-shouldered man, his curly hair cut neatly, his beard trimmed as his fingers delighted over each ivory. But when he looked up, Janet was struck with an intense nostalgia: the kind that felt like she was falling while standing perfectly still.

"No…" The word dropped from her lips.

The Pianist had a similar expression, his lips parted and eyes wide. "Ella?"

"It's a trick," Janet said to herself. "It's not real. It can't be real."

But it was. Time had aged him: paled his light brown hair to gray in places, and struck his face with more wrinkles. But it would be forever Hugh's face, the one she remembered so staunchly in every memory from her childhood until his…

"But you're dead," she squeaked.

He blinked but didn't say anything.

"How is this possible?" The wrench dropped from her fingers. "There were…parts of you…on the tracks. I…took you home."

The creases in Hugh's face deepened. "That wasn't me, sweetheart."

Janet ground her teeth together. "Don't call me that."

He stood up from the piano bench and approached the bar cart. "I had to make you believe. I had to make it look convincing."

Janet shook her head. "Why? What the fuck does that even mean?"

"It was the only thing I could do to protect you." Hugh picked up a decanter from the bar cart, his hand shaking as he poured some into a cut-whiskey glass there. "He had to think you weren't a part of my life anymore. That I wasn't a part of yours."

The words jumbled in Janet's skull, mixing with the pain. "He?"

Hugh knocked back the drink, swallowing before he

made eye contact again. "Steele."

The word sent spikes up and down through her. "Where is he?"

"Not here. He fled as soon as he heard you were coming, the fucking coward." Hugh smirked. "I had hoped it was you, Ella. They all said you went by the name 'Janet' so I wasn't sure but… Look at you."

"Yeah," she bristled. "Take a good look at me, Dad."

He put up a hand. "I knew you were going to be fine. I had every faith in you. After everything I taught you, everything Amos taught you…"

The room was scalding now. How dare he say Amos's name after *this*. Janet reached down and gripped the handle of the wrench. "Did you know that Steele killed Amos? Did you know that when you left me to fucking die on those tracks?"

Hugh poured another glass. "I did. And Steele did it because of me."

Janet almost forgot to breathe. "Because of you? But…"

"Steele isn't a fool. He's calculated. He effectively killed two birds with one stone that day. And poor A—" Hugh choked on the word. He took a sip from his drink. "Poor Amos knew nothing. He had no fucking idea what I'd gotten us into."

"And what was that?" Janet growled.

"Do you remember when we came here when you were a girl?"

She nodded and took a few steps toward the bar cart, wrench still warm in her hand.

"Steele had asked for a meeting with me. He'd heard

about my talents: both musical and magical." Hugh regarded his hands for a moment. "He wanted me for a job. He needed someone to offer a distraction while he infiltrated a room, here in this very hotel. This room in fact. There was someone staying here at the time who was of importance for him, and he needed to gain access to them. He'd have paid me handsomely. I'd have had enough to put your father in a better facility. I'd have had enough to properly take care of us.

"But I knew the stories about Steele. Everyone did. And once you did something for him, there was every likelihood he'd call on you again for something bigger, something worse. I didn't know what he was planning at the time, but I knew it wasn't good. So, I declined his offer…politely, or so I had thought at the time."

Janet stopped in front of the bar cart and grabbed the decanter before he could pour himself another drink. She retreated back a couple steps with it, pulled the top off and tossed it onto a nearby chair.

"You know how strong that is?" he asked her.

Janet took a drink. It hit her mouth and throat like lightning striking an antennae. As it sank into her, its warmth fuzzy and inviting, she stared back at him and said, "Steele doesn't like to be told 'no.'"

Hugh scoffed. "No. He doesn't."

"So." Janet squinted. "He killed Amos not just because of the Man but because of you."

"I had no idea about the doctor's debts with Steele. At the time, I thought he'd killed everyone there as a message to me. I tried to run, Ella. I tried to get us away. But everything fell apart so quickly. There were murders happening in the streets, people fleeing left and right. I should have just taken you away. But, your father…what had happened to him…" Hugh sunk into a nearby armchair. "I was so ashamed and I was so lost without him."

Janet remembered those long nights lying in her sleeping bag in the train tunnel, listening to the tarp flap in the gusts of wind, listening to Hugh crying and shaking next to her. She remembered how gaunt he became as every meal he found he gave to her.

She glanced around the opulent room. "Clearly, you survived."

Hugh's eyes darkened. "I went to Steele to offer myself to him. I was trying to save us. But he didn't just want me: he wanted you, too. He knew you would have my strength someday; you'd have Amos's intellect and both of our magic combined. You'd be a force to be reckoned with and he wanted to control that.

"I couldn't let it happen. So, the only thing I could do was make him believe you were beyond his reach. And as soon as you were orphaned, as soon as the caravan adopted you, you were." A quavering smile crossed his lips.

"Seven years," Janet said hollowly. "I spent seven years wandering this fucking world trying to find my place in it without you. And you were here this whole time?" She held up the wrench. "Do you know how many people's lives I've ended with this? Do you know how many times I brought dead animals back to life just to hear Amos's voice again?"

Hugh's face fell. "What?"

Janet wrenched her jacket sleeve up to show the ink in her arm. "Tattooed his words on my flesh, picked flowers from his grave, and drank my own fucking tears thirteen different times and…" Her throat closed up and tears slipped from her eyes. "I lost him over and over and over." She sniffed. "Tried to bring you back too, but it never worked. Now I know why."

Hugh had stiffened, eyes watering as he beheld her. "How could you? How could you do that to him?"

"Oh, fuck you!" Janet snarled. "How could you abandon me for *this*?" She waved her hands around the room. "You wanted to keep me from becoming Steele's monster and instead I became yours!"

Hugh jumped up from the chair. "I couldn't do anything else. I couldn't let you be corrupted by these people and what they stand for. I've had to kill, too, Ella. I've had to lose myself time and time again for the sake of Steele and his fucking executioners." He scanned her from head to toe. "I imagine they're all dead now."

"You'd imagine correct."

"Well," he chuckled, "Let's get this over with then."

Janet braced herself for the last fight.

THIRTEEN

Crossing the room, Hugh snatched a pair of scissors from a writing desk and casually tossed them on the floor in front of her. Then, he dropped to his knees on the oriental rug.

Janet regarded the scissors with sickness.

"I want you to put them straight into my heart, you understand?" he said, unbuttoning his shirt carefully. "It's important."

Janet's lip curled. "No."

"This isn't a discussion." Hugh parted the shirt to reveal his chest.

Janet swallowed as she took in the number of scars pockmarking his skin. Were they all from Steele? Consequences from the kills he'd been sent to commit? Her resolve hardened and she kicked the scissors away from her. "I didn't kill all of those other fucks just to come up here and—"

"If Steele had offered you a free shot, you'd have taken it," Hugh said. He flung the scissors back across the rug. The handle tapped the edge of her boot.

"You're not him!" she yelled.

"I might as well be!" he rumbled back. "Do you think Steele ever gets his hands dirty? Do you think you ever had a chance to cut him down today, Ella? The night he watched you nearly kill that doctor, he rode out of here like fire in a back-draft. He told us to goad you. He told us you'd come for him if we set you off and that's exactly what happened. Like a long fuse sparking, here you are."

Janet trembled. Every inch of her skin felt dirty, felt manipulated, felt rotten. Dropping the wrench, she reached down and let her fingers slide into the scissor handles. "Did you kill my fox?"

He hung his head. "I didn't. But when the others got back and told me what they'd done, I hated them. Foxes were always Amos's favorites. I should have known it was you just because of that."

"One of the last animals I used to bring Amos's soul back into was a fox," she said, struggling to keep her voice even. "That fox meant peace. It meant hope; something I hadn't had for almost a decade. Something I lost when I lost you, lost him. Steele has ripped that away so many times now. All he had to do was leave me alone."

"I don't think he knows how to," Hugh murmured. "He always gets what he wants."

Janet stared at the scissors, at their sharp point glistening under the lights. Then, at her dad. "Help me," she whispered.

Hugh frowned.

"Help me kill him. Two witches together. We could—"

"I can't, Ella." He nodded at the scissors. "Now, go on. Get it done."

"He won't expect it," she insisted, taking a step toward him. "You owe me this!"

"I can't repay what I owe you," Hugh said. "Not like this. And he will expect it. He has informants in every town all along the east coast. Steele is everywhere. The moment he finds out I've defected; he'll do everything in his power to make sure I am stopped. But you…"

The tears came hot and fast. Ella knew there was nothing to make them stop once they started. She took another step, scissors held horizontal in the space between them.

"You, my dear, are a cannon: overpowering. Even if he knows your coming, he can't stop you. By the time he hears your roar, he'll already be dead." He reached out and took the tips of the scissors between his fingers. He gently pulled her toward him, pulled until the blades touched the hair of his chest above his heart.

Ella felt the metal handle of the scissors slip between her fingers, her heartbeat thrashing in her like the sound of drums. She stared into Hugh's eyes. "Why?" she whispered. "Why did you have to be alive? Why couldn't you stay dead?"

"I will this time, I promise." He wrapped his hand around the blades and steadied them. "And the next time you say your spells, I'll be waiting for you."

Ella took a deep breath, the taste of salt pervading her mouth. "Fuck. Fuck. Fuck. Fuck."

"Come on now," Hugh's voice shuddered. "Do it. Fucking do it—"

Janet screamed as she pulled back and thrust the scissors forward as hard as she could. The blades sunk into his chest like a needle through fabric, the pop of the initial puncture followed by the smooth glide through fat and muscle. Something sheared against the edge of her blades, a rib perhaps before she hit a second pop, headier than the first. The feeling sent shock through her hands all the way up her arms.

Hugh choked, his fingers curling around her grip. A rush of tears cascaded down his face as he gazed into her eyes. Then, he fell back onto the rug.

Blood oozed slowly, its pulse quickening as the seconds passed.

Ella clambered to him and grabbed his hand. She could barely see him through the tears, her own sobs drowning out the sounds of his little gasps.

Hugh put a hand to her chin and lifted it toward the piano. On the holder for the sheet music sat a map with a place circled in red.

She looked back down at him. More and more blood gushed down across his body. "I'm going to kill him." Her fingers tangled in his. "I'm going to end this."

Hugh's other hand cupped the side of her head and he weakly answered, "For Amos." His hand clunked against the carpet and the other stiffened in her grasp as his eyes stared through her.

Death.

Real death.

By her hand.

Janet knelt by Hugh's body as every bit of her folded in on herself, as every memory she cherished of him crashed down over her like ceilings breaking apart floor by floor, the night sky plunging down so it could absorb her.

Who had he really been? Certainly not the man she'd

thought she knew: not this naïve portrayal she'd crystallized in her thoughts for the better part of seven years. No. Hugh wasn't a saint, never wholly good. The mask of this dad who had played with her in the backyard, who had inspired her, who had told her to open up her imagination and let go of rigidity, to trust in their gift.

What horrors had he done over the last seven years to make sure that Steele kept his distance from her? What even was he to her anymore besides a memory of what once was?

It was simple.

He was still her dad.

He had been Amos's love.

And he'd become a monster for them.

What was she then?

Hadn't she done exactly the same thing?

Janet reached up and slid his eyelids closed before finding the energy to stand.

Outside, the night was lightening. Dawn rode the horizon in faint streaks of orange.

At the piano, she plucked the map from its spot and unfolded it. A small paper dropped from it and fluttered down to the rug. She retrieved it and read the scribble, "To Janet. Find the Junco. He'll help you. Steele is in Nothingland. He will be ready for you. Kill him."

Even before he had known it was her, Hugh was going to tell her where to go. He was going to do the right thing.

Shoving the map and the note into her pocket, Janet collected the fallen wrench and the decanter of whiskey and plodded out of the penthouse suite, boots echoing heavily through the space.

FOURTEEN

As Janet walked the train tracks outside of town, the sun rose, its red light setting the purple horizon aglow. No matter where she looked, there were flowers. The heady scent of them made her focus, made her boots connect with pea stone, made her push the pain into the recesses of her mind and think only about the road ahead.

Nothingland. She'd heard tale of it. A place further south along the coast that used to be a tourist trap until the water left it. Now, it was a circus of the damned: a place where men and women went to forget, to wallow in their indulgences and die in a modicum of self-satisfaction.

It made sense Steele would be there: a man who claimed to be a god lording over a land of dreamlike pleasure for those who had nothing left.

As Janet walked, the ground rattled beneath her and the rails sang. She looked up toward the billowing of smoke in the distance.

The fastest way down the east coast was by rail. She didn't have access to a car and didn't know when the next time she'd see a train would be. Their schedules were infrequent and seemed to grow more so by the day.

But home. She'd longed to see it once more, longed to let memories of its innocence dredge over her if only to momentarily forget what she'd endured. To think of Amos washing strawberries at the sink. To think of Hugh as he lay with her in the grass and pointed at clouds in the shapes of cats.

The rails shook harder.

That place had lost its innocence the moment she brought the Man back, the moment she made her choice to go down this road, to follow justice until the very deadly end. That place was no better than Nothingland; a place to forget.

Janet stepped back away from the tracks and searched for the platform: an old wooden staircase that used to let travelers disembark long ago, back when there were still passenger cars. She could see it faintly and forced her legs into a run.

She couldn't forget. She needed to remember. She needed the last memories of Amos and Hugh driving her forward, not the childhood trauma that had guided her so far. She needed the anger. She needed the reality of their loss. Having Amos again only to sacrifice him for her own hatred. Finding Hugh only to realize he'd left her to die.

The platform bobbed closer and closer.

Killing him.

The train whistle screamed.

Watching Amos die over and over in all those animal's bodies.

She ran faster.

Even the Undertaker's sacrifice she'd tuck away in her

head, use it as a whip to lash against herself when she felt like giving up.

It was too late for that now.

The locomotive raged along the tracks and the world shook as it thundered past her.

Janet grabbed the staircase rail and swung onto it, throwing herself up the five or six steps until she hung out on the edge. Cars juddered within a few feet of her as they scraped and hummed. She watched for an approaching carriage with an open door and saw one about four cars down. She leaned back, letting her hands and arms take the brunt of her weight for a moment as she prepared to launch.

It had to be her. Even if the world had gone to hell. Even if there was no coming back from that. She needed to be the one to set it right.

As the third car passed, Janet hurled herself into the air, every muscle screaming with effort. The opening shot out in front of her and her body plummeted down into its cavity, the hay bales inside breaking her fall.

Puffing, she lay there and watched the fields of flowers race away, watched the sun climb and the fiery clouds burn and thought of her fathers.

She thought of the fox playing in the grass.

She thought of her former self scribbling away at her drawings of the night sky.

She thought of Nothingland.

stay tuned for

nothingland

book 3
in the deadlands

coming in December 2024

DEDICATION

This is book is for everyone who supported *Undead Folk*, which was a hugely experimental novelette written during a period of desperation in my life. I've never had a book be as successful as this one and it means the world to me that so many people have identified with its characters and story.

I knew from the onset that Janet's mission wasn't over though I desperately wanted to write a one-and-done piece. The fact that this series continues to go on is a testament to the power of grief and its ability to haunt for a long time.

Nothingland will be the final part in Janet's, Hugh's, and Amos's story and I hope that you will pass along however you feel about these books to others.

Thank you for taking the time to read. I appreciate you.

photo © Colin Borowske 2021

Katherine Silva is an ace Maine horror author, a connoisseur of coffee, and victim of cat shenanigans. Her favorite flavors of the genre mix grief and existentialism which she combines with her love of the New England wilderness in her works. She is a three-time Maine Literary Award finalist for speculative fiction and a member of the HWA and NEHWA. Katherine is also editor-in-chief of Strange Wilds Press. You can find out all about her work at katherinesilvaauthor.com.